Sophisticated Barflies
[& other short plays]

by
Kristen Lazarian

Queen of Wands Publishing

Sophisticated Barflies [& other short plays]
was first produced at the Road Theatre in
North Hollywood, California

ISBN 978-0-578-08887-7

Please note the following:

- No one shall commit or authorize any act of addition or omission by which the copyright of, or the right to copyright, this play may be impaired.

- No one shall make any changes in this play for purposes of production.

- Publication of this play does not imply availability of performance. Both amateurs and professionals who would like to produce this play are advised to apply for written permission before starting rehearsals, advertising or booking a theatre.

- No part of this book may be reproduced, stored in a retrieval system, or transmitted in any form, by any means, now known or yet to be invented, including mechanical, electronic, photocopying, recording, videotaping, or otherwise, without prior consent of the publisher.

Credit Requirements:

Producers of *SOPHISTICATED BARFLIES & OTHER SHORT PLAYS* must give credit to the Author of the Play in all programs and all publicity materials distributed in connection with performances of the Play, and in all instances in which the title of the Play appears for the purposes of advertising, publicity, or otherwise exploiting the Play and production. The name of the Author must appear on a separate line on which no other name appears, immediately following the title and must appear in size of type not less than fifty percent of the size of the title type. The Author must not have name in type smaller than that of the director.

The Plays

SOPHISTICATED
BARFLIES

Sophisticated Barflies

Kristen Lazarian

[JAN & PAM]

Jan and Pam sit at a bar. They face the audience on their respective barstools. Jan and Pam both take a sip of their respective cocktails while they look around the bar.

JAN   Are we looking for men?

PAM   We're looking *at* men.

JAN   There are a lot of men here.

PAM   I'd say it's three to one in our favor.

JAN   I'll take this side of the room. You take that side.

Jan and Pam shift to their respective sides. They are now angled away from each other.

PAM   There's a man.

Jan turns her head to Pam's side to see.

JAN   Where?

PAM   My side.

JAN   The fat man?

PAM   No.

JAN   The tall man?

PAM   No. Over there.

JAN   Bald man?

PAM   That man.

JAN   Short man?

PAM   Not that man.

JAN   Jock man. Drunk man. Foreign man.

PAM   How do you know that man's foreign?

JAN   Bad teeth and a nice suit.

PAM   Italian?

JAN   Transylvanian.

PAM   Bloodsucker.

JAN   Aren't they all?

PAM   Not that man.

JAN   Which man?

PAM   The man I mentioned.

JAN   Toupee man?

PAM   Too Vegas.

JAN   Fake ID man?

PAM   Too adolescent.

JAN   Steroid man?

PAM   Hormonally programmed misogynist. Too hostile.

JAN   Aren't they all?

PAM   That man's not.

JAN   How do you know?

PAM   He's special.

JAN   Show me where he is.

Pam begins to shift to Jan's side of the room, following her man as he walks that way.

PAM   There he goes.

JAN   Be subtle.

PAM   I think he saw me.

JAN   That was such an obvious shift. He thinks you're desperate. Good one.

PAM   Wait—he's looking—don't look—

Jan snaps her head in the direction where Pam looks.

PAM   You're blowing my cover!

JAN   What are you trying to cover?

PAM   My attraction. What else?

JAN   Get brave, Pam.

PAM   Get real, Jan.

JAN   If you're attracted to nipple-ring man, why hide it? Stand on that barstool and make yourself known.

PAM   I'm not interested in nipple-ring man.

JAN   It can't be amputee man.

PAM   Don't—he waved. I'm so embarrassed.

JAN   Amputee man waved? How?

PAM   I'm having heart palpitations over that one man.

JAN   I don't know who you see over there. They're all the same. All something-man.

PAM   That one. That one man.

JAN   Batman. Superman. Secret agent man.

PAM   Now— look quick!

Jan looks quick.

JAN   Gay man.

PAM   Dream man.

JAN   Gay man. I'm telling you—

PAM   No!

JAN   Swear to God.

PAM   You don't know that.

JAN   I can tell.

PAM   Please don't say that. He can't be.

JAN   He's special all right.

PAM   He can't be—

JAN   It's very clear to me.

PAM   No. I can't hear this.

JAN   Too well-groomed.

PAM   Sophisticated.

JAN   Sangria?

PAM   Worldly.

JAN   Skinny cigarettes?

PAM   He asked that girl for one.

JAN   Her boyfriend's smoking Camels.

PAM   She offered.

JAN   It was a test.

PAM   He's polite.

JAN   Too polite.

PAM   He has a deep laugh.

JAN   So did Rock Hudson.

PAM   He's affectionate.

JAN   He's hugging a man!

PAM   They're old poker buddies.

JAN   I'll say.

PAM   He's talking to a woman.

JAN   His sister.

PAM   And he's got rhythm.

JAN   All those years of ballet.

PAM   And good style.

JAN   GQ junkie.

PAM   Probably a journalist.

JAN   He reads his poetry in public.

PAM   Or an actor.

JAN   A men's underwear model at best.

PAM   No wedding ring.

JAN   Very happily single.

PAM   Divorced and fragile.

JAN   I'll give you fragile.

PAM   Maybe he's bi.

JAN   That's optimistic.

PAM   Damn it, Jan!

JAN   What did I say, Pam?

PAM   You're a dream killing bitch!

JAN   (*Aghast*) Excuse me for being honest. If you want to live in la-la-la land be my guest, you delusional bar slut.

PAM   Oh. This is the last time we are ever going out.

JAN   Just because you're desperately driven to unavailable men doesn't mean you have to attack me!

PAM   He's not unavailable! And even if he's gay, I don't care! He'd be fun to shop with!

JAN   But you couldn't bring your dates around him.

PAM   I can't bring my dates around you!

JAN   What is the inference there?

PAM   Let's see. Where to begin? Motorcycle man.

JAN   Nice guy but he never showered.

PAM   Lawyer man.

JAN   Professional, true. But the TV commercial was a bit much.

PAM   Cab man.

JAN   He came and went at annoying hours.

PAM   Psychic man.

JAN   Know it all.

PAM   Florist man.

JAN   Fungus hands.

PAM   I hate you, Jan. You're ruining my life.

JAN   I'm only trying to help you, Pam.

PAM   Then agree with me!

JAN   If you can't hear it like it is—then fine.

PAM   Fine.

JAN   Fine.

PAM   Finish your drink and play with your hair—if you can handle doing two things at once. Just don't talk to me. I'm going over there.

Pam stands to go to the man.

PAM   Macy's is having a sale.

Pam takes a deep breath and goes to take a step, a tentative step.

JAN   See what men do to us? They tear us apart, Pam.

Pam sits down again.

PAM   (*Relieved*) You're so right, Jan.

JAN   If you're lucky, they give you one brief moment of ecstasy and then they push you over the edge, into the abyss. Free fall.

PAM   You've had bad experiences, Jan. It's perfectly understandable that someone who's been dumped as often as you have would be jaded, defensive, and basically wrecked.

JAN   How could you say that—

PAM   It came out quite easily. It's been on the tip of my tongue for months.

JAN   But, Pam, you're my best friend.

PAM   You don't have a monopoly on honesty, Jan.

JAN   And you don't have a monopoly on every single man in the universe!

PAM   Tell that to the gods. I've been blessed.

JAN   You're a stuck up slut, Pam.

PAM   And you're a frigid beast, Jan.

JAN   I can get any man in this bar.

PAM   Depending on how much cash you're carrying.

JAN   I will not let you cripple my self-esteem.

PAM   I didn't even know you *had* self-esteem.

JAN   Fuck you, Pam.

PAM   Fuck you, Jan.

JAN   That flannel man wants me.

PAM   Where?

JAN   There. Don't look.

Pam snaps her head.

JAN   Bitch.

PAM   Who?

JAN   You.

PAM   I know I am the bitch, Jan. Who is this man?

JAN   Right there. That man.

PAM   That is not a man.

JAN   Yes, it is.

PAM   A *wo*-man maybe.

JAN   Is not.

PAM   Small hands.

JAN   Shut up.

PAM   Hips, Jan?

JAN   Please stop, Pam.

PAM   Breasts.

JAN   I don't see breasts.

PAM   Braless even.

JAN   So she's earthy.

PAM   She's the best looking man in this bar.

JAN   I'd do her.

PAM   What are you telling me, Jan?

JAN   I mean if pleasure was all I wanted—

PAM   (*Mumbles*) Pleasure?

JAN   But I'm not looking for pleasure—

PAM   (*Sarcastic*) Really? No—

JAN   I want intimacy. A soul mate. A marriage proposal, 2.8 children, a house in the suburbs and a goldfish named

Sparky. And when if falls apart, I want big, fat alimony checks that arrive on time. Is that too much to ask?

PAM   I've thought about alimony.

JAN   But you won't let a man get too close.

PAM   I'd gladly let a man get close, but you're like a salivating dog blocking my threshold.

JAN   Where the hell is your threshold?! Like I care about your threshold! I didn't even know you had a threshold!

PAM   Don't get vindictive, Jan.

JAN   You should go out by yourself then—if I'm such a barrier to your threshold!

PAM   I'm not going to sit at a bar by myself. That's classless.

JAN   Well, thanks. I feel totally used. And you are classless.

PAM   Well, your jeans are too tight.

JAN   Your roots are too dark.

PAM   Your make-up looks like a Fresh and Fancy head.

JAN   You have hideous bags under your eyes.

PAM   You have a fat ass.

JAN   Your aura's puke green.

PAM   You smell like a yeast infection.

JAN   I hate your hair cut.

PAM   That's not what you said yesterday.

JAN   I lied!

PAM   You're a pathological liar!

JAN   You're pathological!

PAM   Clepto.

JAN   Nympho.

PAM   I hate you, Jan.

JAN   The feeling's mutual, Pam.

PAM   Just stay on your side.

JAN   Fine. You stay on yours.

Beat.

PAM Jan?

JAN Yes, Pam.

PAM I blame our hatred for each other on the penis.

JAN So do I. But I still hate you.

PAM My man is on your side.

JAN Your man has been sticking his tongue down that woman's throat for the last five minutes.

PAM What?

JAN See—

PAM But—

JAN Pig.

PAM But he's gay.

JAN Apparently not *that* gay.

PAM I'm devastated.

JAN You missed your window of opportunity.

PAM She's a tramp.

JAN Terrible features.

PAM Fake tits.

JAN And her purse is a knock-off.

PAM Well. If that's his type.

JAN Who needs him.

PAM Certainly not me.

JAN I wouldn't take him now.

PAM Not even if he begged.

JAN Which he would.

PAM If he wasn't distracted.

JAN See anyone else?

Pam and Jan shift together scoping the area, slowly moving their heads from stage right to stage left.

PAM   They're all the same.

JAN   All something-man.

PAM   Can you ever forgive me for directing all my anger at men toward you?

JAN   Well. Only because I've known you for ten years which is about nine years and eight months longer than you've known any one man.

PAM   I'm so thankful for your consistency and devotion, Jan.

JAN   What man could match that?

PAM   No man at all.

JAN   There's such an indestructible bond between women.

PAM   Because we're more mature.

JAN   I love you, Pam.

PAM   I love you, Jan.

JAN   Let's go rent a movie.

PAM   I am so sick of bars.

JAN   And men in bars.

PAM   Men in bars with business cards.

JAN   Like that's seductive.

PAM   Where are the real men?

Pam begins to look from stage left to stage right. Jan begins to look from stage right to stage left. Finally, they are looking at each other.

JAN   They're in the movies.

PAM   What should we rent?

JAN   Something unbearably tragic.

PAM   I need a good cathartic cry.

JAN   I'm here for you, Pam.

PAM   Thank God, Jan.

JAN   (*Stands to go*) Shall we?

PAM   After you.

> *They exit and—*
> **Black Out**

JOY RIDE

JOY RIDE

Kristen Lazarian

[MISSY & BUDDY & RILEY & TANYA]

The stage space must at first serve as a lobby to a very large building, however, most of the action takes place inside an elevator.

Missy and Buddy are waiting for the elevator. They do not talk because they do not know each other.

*A **DING!** (The bell sound will indicate the elevator doors opening and closing.)*

The doors of the elevator open and Buddy allows Missy to enter before him.

*They are now in the elevator. **DING!** Indicating the doors have closed.*

BUDDY	Going up?
MISSY	Is there any other way to go?
BUDDY	No, I think we're at rock bottom.
MISSY	Yes, I'm going up.

Uncomfortable silence. Both reach to push a floor button at the same time.

BUDDY	Same floor.
MISSY	What?
BUDDY	What a coincidence. We're going to the same floor.

MISSY	(*Flip*) Fate is strange.
BUDDY	Well, put that way—
MISSY	Of all the people in the entire world, you are here and I am here and—no, I don't recall ever meeting you or seeing you before this moment. So, for whatever reason, we are fated to ride this elevator together.
BUDDY	Very interesting take.
MISSY	I don't mean to be metaphysical or anything, but—
BUDDY	But you're right. It's all how you see the world, isn't it?
MISSY	Exactly.
BUDDY	And to think we're going to the same floor even.
MISSY	Not very many people go to the nine hundred and ninety-ninth floor.
BUDDY	No, they certainly don't. Vertigo.
MISSY	I hear that most people who go up there alone end up—you know.
BUDDY	What?
MISSY	You know. Jumping.
BUDDY	No.
MISSY	Oh yes. It's true.
BUDDY	Horrible.
MISSY	It's lonely at the top.
BUDDY	I've heard.
MISSY	I like it on top.
BUDDY	Don't get me wrong. So do I—the rush.
MISSY	Well, we have that in common.
BUDDY	Makes it nice to go there with someone else.
MISSY	Welcome to my ride.
BUDDY	You *were* here first.
MISSY	But, of course, I can share.
BUDDY	I'm getting much better at that.
MISSY	At sharing?

BUDDY	Although, I still think sharing's not what it's cracked up to be.
MISSY	One second you're sharing, the next you're filing bankruptcy.
BUDDY	I know. I've been there.
MISSY	I have an idea. That will be your side and this will be mine.
BUDDY	Good. I won't cross that line. As long as you don't.
MISSY	I won't. No, I won't. I have no desire to.
BUDDY	Perfect.
MISSY	Space is a valuable commodity.
BUDDY	Should be packaged and sold.
MISSY	That's called real estate.
BUDDY	But this is a free elevator.
MISSY	Fortunately, we're mature adults and we've reached a mutually satisfying agreement.
BUDDY	I'm mutually satisfied—as long as you are.
MISSY	Should we draw up a contract?
BUDDY	That won't be necessary, uh—
MISSY	Missy.
BUDDY	Missy. Buddy.
MISSY	Buddy.
BUDDY	Missy.
MISSY	Buddy?
BUDDY	Yes, Missy.
MISSY	I think I've come to trust you.
BUDDY	Careful of trust. We know where that leads.
MISSY	Directly to betrayal. Thank you for reminding me.
BUDDY	Let's not expect too much from each other.
MISSY	You're right. What was I thinking? Trust is irrelevant.
BUDDY	I'll offer you nothing.
MISSY	I'll make no promises.

BUDDY	As long as we have an agreement.
MISSY	You're perfectly free to do whatever you wish in your own space.
BUDDY	As you are.
MISSY	I won't ask. I won't look.
BUDDY	We'll stay blindly respectful.
MISSY	I mean it's not as if we're married.
BUDDY	Or even exclusive.
MISSY	Let alone—committed.
BUDDY	To anything more than the bounds of this 16 square foot area in which you have your own side and I—thank God—have mine.
MISSY	Breathing room.
BUDDY	Plenty.
MISSY	No territorial impulses.
BUDDY	No intimacy.
MISSY	No possessiveness.
BUDDY	Or real connection.
MISSY	We are virtually strangers in an elevator.
BUDDY	So many floors—
MISSY	All these floors, and still strangers.
BUDDY	But so many more to go. So much to look forward to.
MISSY	I feel so alone. I can't touch you.
BUDDY	Touch would be violation of said agreement.
MISSY	Said *necessary* agreement.
BUDDY	At least we're communicating about these things.
MISSY	It makes it much easier.

DING! The elevator stops. Door opens and RILEY enters. The door closes. The elevator continues rising. Now there are three—

| RILEY | (*Pretending surprise*) Missy? |

DING! *The doors have closed.*

MISSY	Riley. How did you know I was here?
RILEY	Kathy and Johnny hinted that you might be on your way up, but just in passing.
MISSY	(*To Buddy*) Kathy and Johnny will do anything to return things to normal.
RILEY	I want things to be normal.
MISSY	Things are normal. I'm getting on with my life. That's what normal people do.
RILEY	But I miss you, Missy.
MISSY	It's too late, Riley. I'm going up and fast. I really don't want you going with me.
RILEY	You can't possibly be happy.
MISSY	I'm not happy. I'm content.

Beat. Realizing—

RILEY	Please don't tell me there's someone else.
MISSY	Vaguely.
RILEY	Someone I know?
MISSY	It's too casual to mention. But promising enough to tell you about it. It's a recent thing really.
RILEY	Really?
MISSY	Really, Riley.
RILEY	This is not what I expected, Missy.

Buddy taps Riley on the shoulder. Riley realizes Buddy is there.

| BUDDY | Excuse me. You're in my space. |

RILEY	Oh, sorry.
MISSY	Riley, my life is none of your business.
RILEY	You can't shut me out like this. Like we never knew each other well enough to see each other naked or share toothbrushes.
MISSY	You used my toothbrush?
RILEY	Just once. When your dog ate mine.
MISSY	That's what killed my dog?
RILEY	That or the rat poison.
MISSY	You used my toothbrush and murdered my dog? And then you have the audacity to come in here and breathe my air? And make me feel guilty because I don't want you back? What's next? Forgiveness? I don't think so, Mister, because the only time you ever appreciated me was when you thought you'd lose me— and now you've lost and I would rather go to the top of this building and take a nose dive then ever be with you again. So get out of my space.

Beat. Buddy pushes a button. **DING!** *And the elevator stops. The door opens and all three stand there in silence looking out. Until finally—*

BUDDY	Nice meeting you.

Buddy makes a move to leave the elevator.

MISSY	Wait! This isn't your floor. Our floor!
RILEY	Our floor? What do you mean—*our* floor.
BUDDY	I think I should go. You have unfinished business.
MISSY	Him? I'm finished with him.
BUDDY	I know what I saw.
RILEY	Did I miss something?
BUDDY	Goodbye, Missy. I'll miss you.

Missy grabs Buddy.

MISSY	Wait! No! Please.
BUDDY	We're touching.
MISSY	So sue me! I can't let you go so soon. I'll have regrets.
RILEY	Him? He's a stranger in an elevator. We have a history together!
MISSY	A history, Riley! A past! A yesterday! That's it. Nothing else. Now get out.
RILEY	What? Really?
MISSY	This is my elevator!
BUDDY	Our elevator.
MISSY	(*Turning to Buddy, faintly*) What?
BUDDY	(*To Riley*) It's our elevator and you're no longer welcome.
RILEY	You will be very sorry for this, Missy.
MISSY	The only thing I'm sorry about is that I didn't get rid of you sooner!

Missy kicks Riley in the butt which thrusts him out of the elevator. The elevator door closes and once again Missy and Buddy are alone.

DING! *They slam faces and kiss.*

BUDDY	Wow.
MISSY	We should have done this many floors ago.
BUDDY	I always wanted to.
MISSY	You did?
BUDDY	I was just—afraid of getting too—
MISSY	Intense?
BUDDY	Serious.

MISSY	But you've changed your mind, haven't you? I mean, you're okay with this now?
BUDDY	I'm afraid of falling in love with you.
MISSY	Who said anything about love?
BUDDY	I didn't. I was just saying—what will this do to our friendship?
MISSY	It wasn't really a friendship.
BUDDY	Of course it was.
MISSY	Friends don't have to make tacit agreements about boundaries.
BUDDY	So you think doing *that* was a defense against *this* happening?
MISSY	Doing *that* was a guarantee that *this* would happen.
BUDDY	I admit the attraction.
MISSY	I had a fascination.
BUDDY	We can't go back.
MISSY	No. We can't.
BUDDY	I'm okay with that. With this.
MISSY	But what is this?
BUDDY	I don't know yet. I only know that I enjoy being with you and—being close.
MISSY	So do I, Buddy.
BUDDY	And it doesn't have to be a love thing.
MISSY	Good. That's exactly right. I don't—pff—love you. I like you a lot. But look, it just so happened that we found ourselves sharing an elevator and there's no need to make it into something that it isn't.
BUDDY	It's fine with me to keep it casual.
MISSY	So we agree. A casual thing.
BUDDY	You're welcome to come over to my side—just let me know before hand.
MISSY	Fine. And you forewarn me and we'll be all right.
BUDDY	Can I come over right now?

| MISSY | I thought you'd never ask. |

Buddy crosses the line and embraces Missy passionately. Missy reciprocates and then she goes limp and becomes unresponsive. He continues awhile until—

BUDDY	What is it?
MISSY	I need to think.
BUDDY	About what?
MISSY	About us. About what we're doing.
BUDDY	There's nothing to think about. It's casual, remember?
MISSY	You have to know something about me, Buddy. I want to light a match but I don't want to start a fire. And this is getting hot.
BUDDY	It can be a casual fire.
MISSY	That's what I need to think about.
BUDDY	Okay. I'll go over to my side. You think.

Buddy is a little irritated. He moves back to his side.

| MISSY | Buddy. |

Buddy doesn't answer.

Buddy.

No answer.

Buddy! Don't do this! I need to talk to you!

| BUDDY | So talk. |
| MISSY | Not from here. Can I come over? |

BUDDY	No.
MISSY	No?
BUDDY	No. I need some space.
MISSY	Oh. Okay. I let you come over here whenever you want but you can't accommodate me in my moment of need. Is that what this is about?
BUDDY	You can't push me away and then blame me for being distant.
MISSY	But I've thought about everything and I know what I want.
BUDDY	And—

*The elevator stops. Another **DING!** Both Missy and Buddy look up at the floor light and then at each other. The door opens and TANYA enters. Tanya is cute and well-endowed. She's chewing bubble gum. She stands between Buddy and Missy.*

Tanya blows an enormous bubble. It pops. Buddy thinks it's adorable. Missy thinks it's annoying.

DING! *The doors close.*

BUDDY	Strawberry?
TANYA	Watermelon.
BUDDY	Smells great.
MISSY	You must've stuffed the whole pack in your mouth.
TANYA	The most I've ever been able to chew is three pieces.
MISSY	She's talented.
TANYA	I'm trying to develop a tongue for all kinds of flavors.
MISSY	Don't you mean—a taste?
BUDDY	Have you ever had Thai food?
TANYA	Yuck. That's dog meat.

BUDDY	No, I know a great place.
TANYA	Yeah?
MISSY	(*Annoyed*) Yeah?
BUDDY	I would love to take you there.
TANYA	Yeah?
BUDDY	Yeah.
MISSY	(*Very annoyed*) Oh yeah?
BUDDY	If you're free.
TANYA	Well, I kinda have to call work to tell them.
MISSY	You kinda have to get the hell out of this elevator before I pull that bubble gum out of your mouth and wrap it around your neck!
TANYA	Geez, lady. What's her problem?
BUDDY	What is your problem?
MISSY	What is my problem? I don't have a problem.
BUDDY	I thought this was a casual thing.
MISSY	Casual is fine. But you can't even be discreet!
BUDDY	Well, you're not giving me a lot of room to keep it from you.
MISSY	Is that my fault? You throw it in my face!
BUDDY	It's innocent.
MISSY	We used to be honest with each other.
BUDDY	How much more honest can I be?
MISSY	I can't believe I could be so blind and stupid. I thought what we had was really special.
TANYA	Why don't you just come with us, lady?
MISSY	That's very generous of you. You obviously know nothing about men—
TANYA	(*To Buddy*) What does she mean?
MISSY	This man wants to expose your tongue to more than Thai food.
BUDDY	That's not true.
TANYA	I've never had Cajun food.

BUDDY	I think you should stay out of this, Missy.
MISSY	I plan to, Buddy.

*Missy pushes the elevator button and it stops. The door opens. **DING!** All three stare out. Missy takes a step toward the door—*

BUDDY	Wait.
MISSY	No, Buddy.
BUDDY	We can work this out.
MISSY	I don't think so.
BUDDY	But we had an agreement. We were going to keep things loose and open.
MISSY	I told you I'd been thinking—I want something more than loose and open. You can have her.

Tanya blows another big bubble and it pops!

BUDDY	I don't want her.
MISSY	But you said—
BUDDY	That's because you never told me.
TANYA	I'm hungry. I want Thai food.
MISSY	Look what you've started.
BUDDY	If you mean it—if you mean that you want to work on this then I don't need to eat Thai food.
MISSY	Yes, I mean it. I love you.
BUDDY	I love you, too, Missy.
TANYA	I had sushi once. It was sickening. But I'm pretty daring generally so here's my number if you ever wanna get dog food.

Tanya hands Buddy a gum wrapper.

BUDDY   I will.

                       Looks at Missy.

               I will not. This will not go any further.

TANYA   Fine with me, Mister. This is my floor any how.
MISSY   Bye now.

                       *Tanya leaves indignantly. Beat. **DING!** The doors
                       have closed.*

MISSY   Don't ever do that to me again.
BUDDY   Honey, I had no idea you'd fallen in love with me.
MISSY   I want to be exclusive.
BUDDY   Committed.
MISSY   Together forever.

                       *Buddy and Missy look out simultaneously and scratch
                       their heads. They think about this—beat.*

MISSY   At least for awhile.
BUDDY   As long as we can stand each other.

                       Beat. Missy begins to lean into Buddy.

MISSY   Buddy, hold me. Coddle me. Take me!
BUDDY   I'd be glad to.

                       *Buddy and Missy begin to fondle and claw at each other
                       passionately. They begin to sink down to the ground.*

MISSY	I am so happy.
BUDDY	It's hard to believe there was a time when we were just strangers in an elevator.
MISSY	It seems like we've been at this for years.
BUDDY	Well, if not years, then many, many floors now.
MISSY	My space is your space.
BUDDY	I can't get enough of you, Missy.

They are all over each other rolling on the elevator floor. Missy ends up on top.

MISSY	Oh God! Oh God!
BUDDY	(*Gasping*) We're almost there! We're almost at the top!
MISSY	Oh God! Oh Goooood!
BUDDY	Oh Missy!
MISSY	We're—we're—we're heeeeere—
BUDDY	The ze—ee—enith—
MISSY	The peak!
BUDDY	Are we—are we peaking?
MISSY/BUDDY	Ohhhhhhh. Whewwwww.

Missy and Buddy separate. They sit on the floor. A couple beats.

BUDDY	You do look a little peaked.
MISSY	Must be the altitude—do you ever think about how far down the shaft below this elevator goes—I mean there's just some little cables holding this thing up—and it's a hell of a drop if—
BUDDY	(*Still recovering*) Ahmm.
MISSY	They snap. My head is spinning.
BUDDY	Ahah.
MISSY	I've never been this high up before.

BUDDY	You haven't?
MISSY	No.
BUDDY	But you told me that you liked the rush.
MISSY	No, you said you liked the rush.
BUDDY	Well, whatever, but you definitely gave me the impression you were more experienced at this.
MISSY	Before or during?
BUDDY	Please don't get paranoid—
MISSY	I am not paranoid I think I'm pregnant.
BUDDY	Come again—
MISSY	I got a little buzz there and then it passed and now I feel light headed and woozy and I think I could even throw up if I thought about it for a minute.
BUDDY	You're not pregnant—

Buddy helps Missy up.

MISSY	I am *not* pregnant. I think I'm sick.
BUDDY	We're high up. You'll be fine.
MISSY	I feel very ungrounded.
BUDDY	That's supposed to be the good part.
MISSY	I want out—hurry—let me out!
BUDDY	Out?
MISSY	Oh my God! Do you feel that? Are we going down?
BUDDY	Down?
MISSY	We're going down.
BUDDY	Are we?
MISSY	It's usually much quicker going down.
BUDDY	Even quicker if the cables snap.
MISSY	I can't breathe, Buddy.
BUDDY	Don't freak out, Missy.
MISSY	I'm claustrophobic—

BUDDY	You are?
MISSY	And you bug.

Beat. Missy didn't meant to say this—then again—

BUDDY	Since when?
MISSY	Since as long as I've known you. I only overlooked it because I thought you were my destiny.
BUDDY	I can't believe I'm hearing this.
MISSY	And I didn't think I'd be saying it so soon, but really, Buddy, I don't have the same feelings as you apparently do.
BUDDY	I give you my space, my body, my heart and that's what I get from you? You bug?
MISSY	Put bluntly.
BUDDY	Tactlessly.
MISSY	I never claimed to be tactful.
BUDDY	And I never saw you as my destiny. I saw you as an opportunity!
MISSY	Quite frankly, Buddy, it turns out I was just killing time.
BUDDY	You're right. We need to get out.
MISSY	As long as we agree.
BUDDY	This can be a mutually satisfying agreement.
MISSY	Possibly.
BUDDY	This is my side—that will be yours.
MISSY	Why is your side bigger?
BUDDY	My side is not bigger.
MISSY	Your side is much bigger.
BUDDY	I really don't care, at this point, Missy. You can have it all. Just let me have this corner, alright?
MISSY	Fine.
BUDDY	Can you breathe now?

MISSY	Much better.
BUDDY	And you're sure about this?
MISSY	Very.
BUDDY	I don't understand what's happened to us.
MISSY	What goes up must go down, Buddy. I would hope that we can be friends. If you can respect my need for space.
BUDDY	You're a space hog, Missy. A glutton for space.
MISSY	We'll never be friends.

*The **DING!** The elevator door opens and they both look out.*

BUDDY	Here we are.
MISSY	That was quick. Thank God.
BUDDY	It's called gravity.
MISSY	An easy let down.
BUDDY	Divine mercy.
MISSY	(*Straining to be kind*) I didn't mean all those nasty things I said up there, Buddy. I will try to remember you with great fondness—
BUDDY	And I'll try to remember you.
MISSY	Thanks for the ride.

Missy and Buddy exit the elevator and go their separate ways.

Beat.

*Tanya enters and gets in the elevator. The **DING!** Riley enters quickly from stage right calling--*

RILEY	Hold that door!

Riley gets into the elevator. He hits a button.

TANYA   Well, look at that. We're going to the same floor.

Tanya smiles seductively at Riley. Riley glances over at her nervously. The doors shut and—

Black out.

SO NICE TO SEE YOU

SO NICE TO SEE YOU

Kristen Lazarian

[BRIAN & HALEY]

A bare stage. Imagine an office.

Brian enters from stage left with a briefcase. He might be wearing a sport coat and tie, but he must be able to take them off quickly. Haley enters from stage right carrying a batch of file folders and a briefcase. She also looks business-like but must be able to change quickly. They pass each other—then stop when realizing—

BRIAN	Helen?
HALEY	Haley—
BRIAN	Haley!
HALEY	Brian! Brian, right?
BRIAN	Yeah! Right! My God! What are you doing here?
HALEY	I have a meeting.
BRIAN	You're kidding! I work here.
HALEY	You're kidding! Wow. It's a great company.
BRIAN	Great company. It is. Bad coffee but great company.
HALEY	Oh no—bad coffee? That's too bad. I think I need some for this meeting.
BRIAN	A sleeper?
HALEY	I expect so, yeah.
BRIAN	You look fantastic.
HALEY	Thanks—the corporate me. You know how that goes.
BRIAN	Well, it becomes you.
HALEY	Thanks.
BRIAN	You're welcome. I mean it.

A happy beat.

HALEY	Well.
BRIAN	Well.
HALEY	So.
BRIAN	So.
HALEY	Anyway.
BRIAN	Any—yeah. The coffee's pretty bad.
HALEY	I'll pass then.
BRIAN	It's lethal.
HALEY	Then I'll definitely pass.
BRIAN	Well, it's really nice to see you. Really.
HALEY	You, too.
BRIAN	I don't want to make you late.
HALEY	You're right. I better go.
BRIAN	Right—*(struggling)* Well, gosh.
HALEY	See you around.
BRIAN	Okay. Sure. Too bad about that coffee, you know. We could've drank some together.
HALEY	Yeah. Too bad. That would've been nice, Brian.
BRIAN	Yeah?
HALEY	Yeah.
BRIAN	Yeah—well, have a great day.
HALEY	You, too. Nice to see you.

Haley continues to walk in the direction she was headed, stage left. Brian watches her go, a couple beats, then he goes in the direction he was headed, stage right.

Now Haley is off stage left and Brian is off stage right.

There could be a short interlude of sorts, to allow for minor costume changes. Mall music plays in the backdrop.

Haley reenters from stage left. She is carrying a department store shopping bag. She looks more casual, relaxed. Brian then enters from stage right. He also carries a shopping bag from some sort of tech store.

Imagine a shopping mall.

HALEY	Brian—hi.
BRIAN	Oh, Haley.
HALEY	What a coincidence.
BRIAN	Yeah, shopping?
HALEY	My sister's birthday.
BRIAN	My sister just had a birthday.
HALEY	Really?
BRIAN	My younger sister.
HALEY	I didn't know you had a sister.
BRIAN	Two actually.
HALEY	I only have one. Older.
BRIAN	Yeah? I'm the middle.
HALEY	Yeah. I'm the younger.
BRIAN	Right—I got that.

Trying to be polite.

HALEY	Anyway.
BRIAN	Family's a good thing.
HALEY	Mine's dysfunctional.
BRIAN	But—hey. You know, that keeps things interesting.

HALEY	My sister used to beat me in my sleep.
BRIAN	You don't say—
HALEY	I only buy her presents so she'll love me.
BRIAN	(*Trying compassion*) Listen, if you—
HALEY	I know I'm a fool. You can't buy someone's love. But I'll do anything to stop the nightmares, the sleepless nights of terror and tossing.
BRIAN	Uhhh.
HALEY	There are times when I really hate myself, Brian, and I am *not* making this up.
BRIAN	If you ever need to talk about it—
HALEY	(*Now emotional*) I'm sorry. This is very difficult for me to talk about. I have to go.

Haley exits quickly in the direction she was headed, stage right. Brian watches her slightly concerned and confused and then exits himself, stage left.

Haley is now off stage right. Brian is off stage left.

Another interlude. Classical music plays lightly. Slight costume changes are necessary to indicate another day.

Haley enters from stage left. She carries a cup of coffee in one hand and has a newspaper in the other. Brian enters from stage right. He's looking at his wallet, counting his money.

Imagine a coffee house.

HALEY	(*Seeing him first*) Brian. What do you know.
BRIAN	Haley. I'm seeing you everywhere.
HALEY	I didn't know you came here.

BRIAN	First time in months. Are you sleeping better, by the way?
HALEY	What?
BRIAN	Your sister—the nightmares.
HALEY	Oh. Pff. That.
BRIAN	I was concerned.
HALEY	I'm much better. She found God and apologized for everything.
BRIAN	I'm glad to hear it. Nothing like God to put things in order.
HALEY	She's pretty fanatical.
BRIAN	Oh?
HALEY	But not violent. So that's good.
BRIAN	Well good to hear. So I woke up craving one of those cold mochas they have here.
HALEY	Iced mocha.
BRIAN	Iced. Right.
HALEY	They're really good.
BRIAN	My favorite. Can I get you anything?
HALEY	No, I'm fine. Thanks.
BRIAN	You come here a lot?
HALEY	I live down the street.
BRIAN	No.
HALEY	Yeah.
BRIAN	I live *up* the street.
HALEY	Wow. We're neighbors even. Who knew?
BRIAN	Small world.
HALEY	*What* a small world.
BRIAN	Yeah. Can you believe that?
HALEY	Amazing.
BRIAN	I like your hair. You did something—
HALEY	No. It's the same. It's exactly the same. But thanks.

BRIAN   (*Growing discomfort*) Well.

HALEY   (*Lifting her cup*) Beats the coffee at your office.

BRIAN   Yes! Right! It does.

                 Realizing this is going nowhere.

HALEY   Nice to see you, Brian.

BRIAN   Thanks, you too.

                 A beat or two. Both are about to speak—but no,
                 nevermind.

HALEY/ BRIAN Have a—

                 They laugh.

HALEY   See you around.

BRIAN   Right. See ya.

                 Haley walks off, stage left. Brian hits his head a couple
                 times, realizing he's missed an opportunity yet again.

                 Brian walks off, stage right.

                 Another interlude. Pop music plays softly in the
                 background.

                 Haley enters with a small grocery shopping cart, which
                 she carries. Brian enters with a bag of groceries. Haley
                 notices Brian first.

                 Imagine a grocery store.

HALEY	Oh shit.

Haley quickly turns away from Brian and fixes her lipstick. She turns back—

Brian!

BRIAN	Haley!
HALEY	Hi.
BRIAN	Hey.
HALEY	This is becoming a bad habit.
BRIAN	No. No, I was hoping I'd run into you.
HALEY	(*Hopeful*) Really?
BRIAN	Yeah. You know I was sick for two days after I drank that iced mocha.
HALEY	(*Disappointed*) Oh.
BRIAN	Oh, God. It was disgusting. I was puking this yellow guck and I was achy and then the chills.

Not what she wanted to hear.

HALEY	Ahah.
BRIAN	I'm thinking it was food poisoning. Old mocha maybe.
HALEY	(*Irritated*) Wow. I'm sorry about that.
BRIAN	Did you get sick?
HALEY	No. I was fine.
BRIAN	Isn't *that* weird?
HALEY	You probably had the flu.
BRIAN	Yeah, I guess. Or something! I hope I didn't breathe on you that day.

HALEY	Well, if you did, I was fine.
BRIAN	Thank God. You didn't want what I had.
HALEY	You look healthy.
BRIAN	Well, yeah. I am *now*. But—
HALEY	Really knocks you out.
BRIAN	Oh, it was terrible. Glad to be back though.
HALEY	Good.
BRIAN	Still a little queasy, but I think it's passing.
HALEY	You should get some carrot juice.
BRIAN	Really? What aisle would that be in?
HALEY	I have no idea really. I think it's in the back.
BRIAN	That back?

Brian points past Haley, toward stage right.

HALEY	That back.
BRIAN	I'm there.
HALEY	Okay.
BRIAN	Thanks.
HALEY	Sure.
BRIAN	Which way are you—
HALEY	(*Indicates stage left*) This way. Bagels.
BRIAN	Oh. That's too bad.
HALEY	But it was nice to see you.
BRIAN	You too, Haley.

As they are parting, there is something more pathetic about this goodbye.

HALEY	Take care, Brian.
BRIAN	Take care, Haley.

HALEY	Get well.
BRIAN	I will. Stay well.
HALEY	I will.
BRIAN	Bye.
HALEY	Bye bye.

Haley exits now stage left. Brian exits stage right.

Music: Something upbeat like "One Mint Julep." The lights change to evoke a more night time party feel.

Imagine a party.

Haley enters from her side, stage left. She has a drink in her hand—champagne—and she's laughing politely as if someone just told her a joke. She faces stage left and calls off to someone invisible—

HALEY (*Lifting her full champagne glass*) I have one thanks!

From stage right, our man Brian enters with a tumbler full of scotch. He's looking more relaxed but a little dazed. Haley turns just in time to be face to face with him.

BRIAN	Unbelievable.
HALEY	What do you know.
BRIAN	Haley.
HALEY	Brian. I didn't know you knew the Hallams.
BRIAN	I went to college with their son.
HALEY	Jeff?
BRIAN	John.
HALEY	Oh. Jeff was best friends with my ex-boyfriend.

BRIAN	Joe?
HALEY	Yes! Don't tell me you know Joe.
BRIAN	No. I overheard Jeff tell John that he wasn't coming because you'd be here.
HALEY	That's interesting. So—
BRIAN	So—I would think it would be a relief.
HALEY	*Such* a relief.
BRIAN	He sounds like a jerk.
HALEY	That would be Joe. The epitome of insecurity. You can see why we didn't last.
BRIAN	Bad breakup?
HALEY	The break up was a cake walk compared to the relationship.
BRIAN	A long one?
HALEY	Beyond tedious.
BRIAN	Sounds familiar.
HALEY	That's right. Someone told me you went through a divorce.
BRIAN	Get this—we missed the deadline for an annulment by two days. Two days!
HALEY	Well, what difference does it make. So it looks better on paper. The *loss* is still the same.
BRIAN	It was very mutual and friendly.
HALEY	See, that's so great. My ex-boyfriend is a sociopath.
BRIAN	That must've been rough.
HALEY	Good thing I'm resilient.
BRIAN	If you can get out with as little damage as possible then you're good.
HALEY	You're so right. But it sounds like it was easy for you.
BRIAN	Well, at first. Then she broke down.
HALEY	Delayed reaction, I guess.
BRIAN	God, the begging and crying really grated.
HALEY	She still wants you back?

BRIAN	Desperately. Yeah.
HALEY	How sad for her.
BRIAN	Maybe—but I can't think about *her* feelings. I'm happy with my life. I want to date. Get back out there. Meet people. You know, meet people I can feel passionate about.
HALEY	Oh.
BRIAN	We deserve that in this life.
HALEY	Yes. I agree.
BRIAN	I—I want you to know, that I really enjoy talking to you.
HALEY	That's nice. Thanks.
BRIAN	It's hard to get used to—I don't know—

Breaks off unsure.

HALEY	What? Don't—come'on. What were you saying?
BRIAN	It's hard to get back into the scene.
HALEY	Yeah, it is a scene.
BRIAN	And feel comfortable with people—women—again. I've been out of it for so long.
HALEY	I understand. I do.
BRIAN	Yeah?
HALEY	This is the first party I've been to in months and months and months.
BRIAN	That long?
HALEY	Yes. It's that *thing*. Starting over. It's difficult. I think that's why people stay in pathetic, self-destructive relationships forever. It's the fear of *this*.
BRIAN	It's true.
HALEY	But it's nice to get out. It's time for me.
BRIAN	Me, too. I hear *that*.
HALEY	You look great.

BRIAN   Thanks. Thanks a lot.

HALEY   I wish I knew you knew all these people I know.

BRIAN   I know! We could've come here together.

Beat. Realization.

HALEY   We could've.

Haley wonders if he's sincerely interested.

BRIAN   Oh well.

Haley figures he's not.

HALEY   Yeah. Next time.

BRIAN   Right. Did I already tell you how nice you look
            tonight?

Then again—

HALEY   No. But thanks.

BRIAN   No really.

He is interested.

HALEY   Thanks.

BRIAN   I haven't had sex in awhile. Couple months.

Too interested.

HALEY   Oh? Me either. At *least* that.

Suddenly awkward.

BRIAN	I feel like I can talk to you about these things.
HALEY	And you can.

Uncomfortable beat.

BRIAN	Well.
HALEY	Well.
BRIAN	What are you drinking?
HALEY	Champagne.
BRIAN	Scotch.
HALEY	A scotch man.
BRIAN	Every now and then—
HALEY	Potent.
BRIAN	I am—I mean, it is. *(Covering)* We should do something sometime, you know. Go on a cruise or something— sometime.
HALEY	A cruise? Wow.
BRIAN	I mean, cruise around. Hang out. Talk and hang out.
HALEY	Yeah.
BRIAN	Or we could go on a real cruise, if you're not seasick.
HALEY	Not right now, I'm not.
BRIAN	If you don't *get* seasick.
HALEY	I think they have medication for that.
BRIAN	They do. There you go.
HALEY	Perfect. So—
BRIAN	So—
HALEY	So maybe sometime we could go on a cruise.
BRIAN	What are you doing later?
HALEY	Later? Tonight? I don't know. I came with a bunch of people.

BRIAN	Oh.
HALEY	I drove them. So.
BRIAN	Ah. Okay.
HALEY	Well.
BRIAN	Well.
HALEY	So—maybe I'll see you around.

Brian is now feeling inappropriately rejected.

BRIAN	(*Cool facade*) Maybe. Yeah. Whatever.
HALEY	(*Irritated*) Okay, Brian. You take care.
BRIAN	Okay. I will, Haley. Hey, you stay away from sociopaths now.
HALEY	I will. Thanks.
BRIAN	Nice seeing you again.
HALEY	Goodbye, Brian.

Haley exits stage right, crossing Brian who exits stage left.

Sound of airplane landing. In this interim, both Haley and Brian might want to throw on overcoats.

Haley enters from stage right, Brian from stage left. Both are pulling small suitcases.

Imagine an airport.

Haley sees Brian first. She quickly puts on sunglasses. As they get closer, Brian realizes it is Haley. They both keep walking past—

HALEY	Hi, Brian.

BRIAN   Haley, hello.

> *They pass each other and then both of them stop before walking off. They are about to turn to each other—but why?*

HALEY   Forget it.

BRIAN   Nevermind.

> *Haley and Brian both exit quickly and—*
>
> **Black Out**

RECOVERY

RECOVERY

Kristen Lazarian

[NICKY & JESSICA]

A dark stage. Over the LOUD SPEAKERS we hear—

VOICE   **Three hours after Nicky has been dumped.**

> *Lights come up on Nicky's apartment. The living room is empty.*

> *A knock on the door. The knocking continues and becomes more frantic. Finally Jessica enters looking concerned and distraught.*

JESSICA   Nicky? Nicky? Where are you? I rushed over as soon as I heard your message—Nick? Nicky, come out here!

> *A GUNSHOT is heard offstage. Jessica freezes in horror. Then she paces, doesn't know what to do. She is looking for the phone.*

JESSICA   Nnnn—Nick—Nicky—oh God, oh God, oh God, oh God, Nicky! Somebody call the police! Police! Help me. Oh God, help me. Please help!

> *Nicky enters the living room from the bedroom which is stage left. She looks half-dead, depressed, and despondent. She wears a terry cloth robe and her makeup is running down her face. She's been crying. She holds the gun in one hand and some tissues in the other. She sobs.*

NICKY	I missed.
JESSICA	Oh thank God.
NICKY	For what?
JESSICA	Put the gun down, Nicky, okay?
NICKY	(*Waving the gun*) Look at me—looooook—
JESSICA	Can I have the gun?
NICKY	Do you promise to shoot me?
JESSICA	Honey, come on. Max is *not* worth all this.

> *Nicky cries even harder now. She's devastated. She gives Jessica the gun.*

NICKY	Will you shoot *him* then?
JESSICA	You're just upset.
NICKY	No shit.
JESSICA	You don't want to die.
NICKY	Yes, I do.
JESSICA	Think of all the people you'd upset.
NICKY	I don't care about all-the-people.
JESSICA	All-the-people care about you.
NICKY	(*Bawls*) But *Max* didn't care about me. I wanted *Max* to care about me.
JESSICA	I know. I know you did.
NICKY	Five fucking years of my life.
JESSICA	I know.
NICKY	I gave him everything!
JESSICA	I know.
NICKY	And he took it!
JESSICA	Yes, he did.
NICKY	I'm a big zero thanks to him.
JESSICA	No, you're not.

NICKY	Even when everyone said he was a loser and remember when you said he was a manipulator—
JESSICA	I remember.
NICKY	Well, even then I stood by him.
JESSICA	You did.
NICKY	Because there were a lot of good times—
JESSICA	Probably some.
NICKY	There were some good times when no one else was around.
JESSICA	Okay.
NICKY	I thought we were doing okay. We were working on it, you know. And things were just about to get good. I could feel all the good stuff coming.
JESSICA	Maybe.
NICKY	But he panicked! He couldn't take it. And—and he told me in a text! A text, Jessica!
JESSICA	He was never very confrontational.
NICKY	I really liked that about him.
JESSICA	I am so sorry. This is awful.
NICKY	It is awful. He's awful. Max is an awful, cruel human being. How do I get him back?
JESSICA	You don't want him back. Just give it time.
NICKY	There is no time. I don't have any time.
JESSICA	Of course you do. You'll meet someone else.
NICKY	I won't.
JESSICA	Sure you will.
NICKY	I will not.
JESSICA	I promise you.
NICKY	I'm gonna end up like that pathetic old woman who was found dead in her wedding dress because she was stood up at the altar like a hundred years before.
JESSICA	Who?
NICKY	You know—Dickens.

JESSICA	Miss Havisham? I don't think she was dead.
NICKY	She wasn't even dead?
JESSICA	No, she was just old and decrepit.
NICKY	That's gonna be me!
JESSICA	You're nothing like that.
NICKY	Yet.
JESSICA	And thank God. Really, Nicky. Thank God, you never married him.
NICKY	Easy for you to say. You have a perfect marriage. And there have been many times I have been very suspicious of your so-called perfect marriage, believe me.
JESSICA	It's not always perfect.
NICKY	Is it falling apart?
JESSICA	I don't think so.
NICKY	Then it's pretty much perfect.
JESSICA	You'll find something better.
NICKY	(*Morbidly*) It'll have to be in the afterlife, Jessica. There is nothing to live for.
JESSICA	Don't say that.
NICKY	(*Sobs*) I don't know what.
JESSICA	You can start with yourself.
NICKY	Who?
JESSICA	There, there. This too shall pass.

Lights begin to fade.

NICKY	Where's my tissue?

Jessica hands her the box off the coffee table.

JESSICA	Here you go.

Nicky blows her nose.

JESSICA   There you go. Just let it all out.

And black out.

The stage is black. The voice is heard over the loudspeaker.

VOICE   **Three days later.**

Nicky is on the couch, sprawled out with a box of tissue. She flips through songs on a music player until she lands on an easy listening station playing a classic and overly sentimental love song. She sniffles. Jessica enters.

JESSICA   Look at you. Right where I left you three days ago.

NICKY   I know. I should've been married and had a family by now.

JESSICA   Getting dressed would be a start.

NICKY   Then I'd have to shower.

JESSICA   Really, Nicky. It's time to get out.

NICKY   I can't.

JESSICA   And why is that?

NICKY   For one—

JESSICA   You've been dumped.

NICKY   That and *Pillow Talk* is on in a half hour.

JESSICA   Record it.

NICKY   Max always recorded things. He never left me very much room on the DVR.

JESSICA   You cannot go on like this. If you'd get up and get dressed and get outside perhaps you'd feel a little less sorry for yourself.

NICKY	I resent you saying that. I really resent it.
JESSICA	So, resent it.
NICKY	Don't you dare rush me, Jess. I am *not* getting over him in three days. And thanks so much for your compassion and understanding.
JESSICA	All this sadness is making me anxious.
NICKY	Is this about you? I don't think this is about you.
JESSICA	How can this come as such a shock?
NICKY	I am not in shock. I am mourning.
JESSICA	(*Mumbling*) Well, we've all been mourning this relationship.
NICKY	What?
JESSICA	Nothing.
NICKY	Who is we?
JESSICA	Everyone. Pretty much everyone. The universe. We've all been surrounded by negative energy—and I can put a name to that energy. I think that name is Max.
NICKY	He's not the anti-christ.
JESSICA	No, not enough charisma.
NICKY	He was brooding—
JESSICA	Depressive.
NICKY	Romantic.
JESSICA	Is that what you call those roses from Seven-Eleven?
NICKY	I loved him.
JESSICA	That's fine. You go on mourning.
NICKY	And it could take me a long time.
JESSICA	I'm only trying to help you.
NICKY	It could take me years, in fact.
JESSICA	I just want you to get better.
NICKY	It'll probably take lifetimes.
JESSICA	Dammit, Nicky! I will not let you do this. We're going to the mall.
NICKY	I am *not* going to the mall.

JESSICA	New clothes? You love clothes.
NICKY	I love my old clothes. I love the clothes he touched.
JESSICA	Then we'll get house things.
NICKY	It won't fill the void. It'll just remind me of him. There's that toaster I bought to get over Max. There's those stupid animal salt and pepper shakers I bought to make me laugh. There's that Monet print—just because Max hates Monet. We both hate Monet. See?
JESSICA	See what?
NICKY	See how much we had in common? We were perfect together.
JESSICA	Because you both hate Monet?
NICKY	We agreed all the time. But no—he couldn't see it the same way.
JESSICA	He lost the best thing he'll ever have.
NICKY	Do you think he knows?
JESSICA	He will eventually.
NICKY	Eventually?
JESSICA	Why don't we go for a walk?
NICKY	We used to walk places together. Well, usually he'd walk about three feet in front of me, but he had a cute butt.
JESSICA	I'll take you to lunch.
NICKY	We met in a restaurant. Actually, I was eating there and he just came in to use the restroom because he wasn't sure he'd make it all the way home.
JESSICA	What if I fly you to Paris for a week?
NICKY	What if he texts?

Beat.

He's not gonna text.

Beat.

He won't text.

JESSICA	I doubt he'll text.
NICKY	Because he's seeing someone else?
JESSICA	I don't know. I only know he's a jerk. He doesn't deserve you.
NICKY	I doubt he'll text, too.
JESSICA	I'll be back.
NICKY	Okay.

Jessica starts to leave.

Wait.

JESSICA	What?
NICKY	Will you check my cell phone?

Jessica grabs Nicky's cell phone.

JESSICA	Why?
NICKY	Is it on?
JESSICA	Yes, it's on.
NICKY	Set it down very carefully.

Jessica sets it down.

JESSICA	I'm going shopping by myself.

Waving her tissue and not listening—

NICKY   Have fun.

JESSICA   Can I get you anything?

NICKY   No.

JESSICA   More tissue?

NICKY   No. I'm fine.

JESSICA   Anti-depressants?

> *Lights begin to fade to black.*

NICKY   (*Not hearing Jessica*) No, thanks.

JESSICA   Okay, Nicky. Sleep it off.

NICKY   Okay.

> *Nicky snuggles into the couch. Jessica exits and after a couple sobs from Nicky—*

Black out.

> *Through the darkness, we hear—-*

VOICE   **Three weeks after Nicky's break-up.**

> *Nicky's apartment. It looks much cleaner. There are, however, a stack of unpaid and unopened bills on a table.*

> *There is a rattle at the door. Jessica enters with many shopping bags. She sets them down around the couch and coffee table. Nicky straggles in behind her. She looks slightly dazed, confused.*

> *While Nicky goes on and on, Jessica begins pulling things out of the bags. She hands them to Nicky who tosses*

everything Jessica hands her to the side, without even noticing what she holds.

Nicky's conversation with herself has been going on for some time and Jessica has clearly tuned her out.

NICKY   (*Entering mumbling, hardly audible*) I don't get it. One day we're drinking wine in the bathtub designing the house we're gonna build together and the next—the next— he sends me a text—

        Jessica hands her a new sweater out of the bag. Nicky tosses it aside.

He says—like it's no big deal—like he's telling me he can't make it for lunch—

        Nicky tosses a new pair of pants.

Sorry, Nick. Can't make the relationship. I need to grow. G-R-O, by the way—

        She tosses a shoe box and the shoes fall out.

I was supposed to help him do that. That's what I was there for. That's what you're supposed to do in a relationship.

        Jessica hands Nicky animal salt and pepper shakers—thinks a second—and decides not to let Nicky toss these.

NICKY   Where are we?

JESSICA   Home.

NICKY   The Home Store?

JESSICA	Your home, Nick.
NICKY	There's no heart like home. Place sweet place. Who's home?
JESSICA	Yours.
NICKY	It looks different.
JESSICA	I had it cleaned. Are you sure you don't need therapy?
NICKY	Why would I pay someone hundreds of dollars to tell me things I don't want to hear?
JESSICA	They'll tell you what you *need* to hear.
NICKY	You do that, Jess. And I find it annoying.
JESSICA	I'll send you my bill.
NICKY	I'll add it to my collection.

Jessica is looking at Nicky's unopened mail.

JESSICA	Oh God, Nicky. Speaking of bills.
NICKY	Don't speak.
JESSICA	Is this all your mail?
NICKY	I don't know.

Jessica goes to Nicky on the couch.

JESSICA	Look what's happened to you. Is he really worth destroying your credit rating?
NICKY	It's an obvious metaphor for my emotional bankruptcy.
JESSICA	It's irresponsible.
NICKY	The only piece of mail I want is an email begging me back. I am so sorry, Nick. I didn't have the maturity or strength of character to love you like a real man. But after weeks of introspection and not to mention the self-help books, fasting and prayer—I have come to the conclusion that you are too wonderful to live without.

JESSICA	He'd misspell conclusion.
NICKY	Or introspection.
JESSICA	Or the.
NICKY	He had other good qualities. One, in particular.
JESSICA	So you had good sex. That's certainly not everything.
NICKY	Until you stop having it.
JESSICA	I have been telling you for weeks to go have it.
NICKY	Go have sex?
JESSICA	Yes.
NICKY	With a stranger?
JESSICA	Sure.
NICKY	That's not me.
JESSICA	Then date someone first and then have sex.
NICKY	I'm not ready.
JESSICA	Alright. Are you having it with yourself?
NICKY	Sex?
JESSICA	Yes. Sex.
NICKY	Oh, please.
JESSICA	You must be.
NICKY	I should get some sort of toy.
JESSICA	You should.
NICKY	Jessica, I don't want a toy!
JESSICA	You don't have any? It's actually better.
NICKY	How long have you been married?
JESSICA	Nine years.
NICKY	(*Concerned*) And it's better when you—
JESSICA	Yes, mm hmm. I still—you know.
NICKY	Really?
JESSICA	It's nothing more than a sign of a very healthy libido. You want to borrow something?
NICKY	Of yours? God, no.

Beat.

JESSICA	You will be fine.
NICKY	After some time goes by.
JESSICA	Yes, exactly.
NICKY	Things will work out.
JESSICA	I know they will.
NICKY	And maybe he'll send an email. Who knows.

Beat. Lights begin to fade to black.

JESSICA	No, I don't think so.
NICKY	You could lie.
JESSICA	You've been lied to enough.
NICKY	You're right. Where are my bills?

And black out.

The stage is black. The voice comes up over the loudspeaker.

VOICE   **Three months after being dropped by Max.**

Nicky's apartment. From outside her front door, we hear Nicky talking to someone.

We do not see who she is talking to.

Nicky does not see that Jessica has come out from the bedroom. She stands somewhere behind Nicky and

eavesdrops, hopeful at first, but her growing
disappointment becomes apparent.

NICKY   Well. Thanks. I had a really—really—really—a really great time. I did.

Smiling, nodding—a beat.

Again? This? Do this again, you mean?

Smiling, nodding—a beat.

Come in? No! Don't come in!

Smiles again, nods—

I mean, it's such a mess in here. Busy, busy me. Who has time to clean? I hardly have time for these sorts of outings—dates. Whatever this was.

Nodding, more agitated.

Thanks so much. No, really. Great time. Jessica said such great things about you.

Her head hurts from nodding.

What? Of course I'm over Max. Really. So, okay. Bye bye.

Nicky slams the door in his face. She turns—only to have Jessica in her face.

NICKY	AAAHHH!!!
JESSICA	Hi there.
NICKY	You scared me!
JESSICA	Sorry.
NICKY	No, don't be sorry. I'm so glad you're here. Now I don't have to drive all the way to your house to beat the shit out of you!
JESSICA	Did something go wrong?
NICKY	Slightly.
JESSICA	I can't imagine what. Did you screw it up because he's perfect!
NICKY	Don't you get it? I'm too damaged for perfect.
JESSICA	Well, you don't have to tell him that.
NICKY	Oh, he knows. Trust me.
JESSICA	You didn't.
NICKY	I never shut up. I talked about Max the entire time. The ups, the downs, the ins, the outs—
JESSICA	The ins and outs?
NICKY	In graphic detail.
JESSICA	How graphic?
NICKY	Very!
JESSICA	You'll just have to try again. Obviously he wants to take you out. I heard your pleasant little exchange.
NICKY	He was being polite.
JESSICA	Not a bad quality.
NICKY	I think he's a real gentleman. He sat there the entire time and he never spoke. *(Thinking)* He *is* perfect.
JESSICA	He's a great guy. I've known him for months.
NICKY	Just months?
JESSICA	I'm not usually wrong about these things.
NICKY	The last thing he wants to do is see me again. I was taxing.
JESSICA	Damn it, Nicky.

NICKY	Basically obsessing.
JESSICA	How could you?
NICKY	I am not ready for this.

Knock at the door.

Oh my God, hide me!

JESSICA	Do you think that's him?
NICKY	I don't know. Answer it!

Nicky goes off into her bedroom and Jessica goes to the door. Jessica opens the door. The "date" is standing there, though we don't see him.

JESSICA   Well, hi! What a surprise. What are you doing here—again? *(Jessica smiles and nods)* Nicky? No—she—uh—had to step out. *(More smiles and nods)* I was just in the neighborhood. Thought I'd stop by.

We see a man's hand extend to Jessica. He holds Nicky's sunglasses. Jessica takes them.

Thank you. How sweet you are, coming all the way back here just to give her these.

Jessica looks at the glasses. She hands them back to him.

You know, maybe it would be better if you gave these sunglasses to Nicky yourself, at some other time, say Saturday night? *(Smiles)* Of course she can.

Nicky comes out from the bedroom and hangs back to listen.

Don't be silly. She'd love to. What? Oh, it was nothing! I see two lonely people, I do what I can.

Jessica closes the door. Nicky is standing there, which surprises her.

AAHH!!

NICKY	You encouraged him!
JESSICA	No, I did not!
NICKY	Why'd you say, she'd love to? I'd love to what? What would I love to do?
JESSICA	Get your sunglasses.
NICKY	I left my sunglasses?
JESSICA	He was bringing them back. Because he's polite, remember?
NICKY	Where are they?
JESSICA	What?
NICKY	My glasses.
JESSICA	He has them.
NICKY	He came over here to tell me that he has my sunglasses but he's not giving them to me? Until what? Until what exactly, Jessica?
JESSICA	I thought Saturday night would be a good time to get them back.
NICKY	No.
JESSICA	Oh, Nicky!
NICKY	You have to stop this. I will be fine. I need you to trust that I will be fine. Yes, Max hurt me very much. Yes, I wanted Max to be different. Yes, I am getting tired of having sex with myself—but you have to let me work through it in my own way.

Beat.

So find another problem to fixate on.

Beat.

Max has only been out of my life for three months. This is completely post-relationship appropriate.

JESSICA	You're probably right.
NICKY	Now go get my sunglasses.
JESSICA	Now?
NICKY	And then you can explain to him why I'm not going out with him on Saturday night.
JESSICA	Ugh. Fine. Are you sure?

Lights begin to fade to black.

NICKY	Positive.
JESSICA	Okay.
NICKY	Okay.
JESSICA	He *is* perfect.

Black out.

Black stage. The man's voice returns over the loudspeaker.

VOICE   **Nine months and three days have now transpired.**

Lights come up on Nicky sitting on her couch. She is dressed up. She is holding a compact and putting on lipstick.

Knock at her door.

NICKY   Come in, Jess.

Jessica enters.

JESSICA   Ready?

NICKY   Almost.

JESSICA   Look at you. You look like the old Nicky.

NICKY   The new and improved Nicky.

JESSICA   Much improved.

NICKY   How much?

JESSICA   Much.

NICKY   That much?

JESSICA   No, you didn't need *that* much. Just a little.

NICKY   How little?

JESSICA   Will you please shut the fuck up. We gotta go.

NICKY   Well, it takes some time to improve myself—*much*.

JESSICA   You look beautiful. And you're doing my husband a big favor by coming out tonight. The place needs to look full.

NICKY   Just remember I hate bars and I won't be any fun.

JESSICA   I remember.

NICKY   You do?

JESSICA   I expect it.

NICKY   You do?

JESSICA   But you're still my best friend and I love you.

NICKY   You don't think I'm fun?

JESSICA   Sometimes you're fun.

NICKY   Who is this band your husband is promoting?

JESSICA	I don't know—Something Band. It's all women. They're like a mom band. They have lavender hair.
NICKY	I'm sorry, *what?*
JESSICA	It's a statement.
NICKY	Did you say they have lavender hair?
JESSICA	In their publicity photos, they do.
NICKY	A subtle lavender or shocking sort of purpley lavender?
JESSICA	You're stalling and we're leaving.
NICKY	Go without me.
JESSICA	I'm not going without you. I promise all you have to do is sit there.
NICKY	I should be really good at sitting there since I'm no fun.
JESSICA	You're just more introspective.
NICKY	I don't want to be introspective.
JESSICA	Then let's pretend it's the old days—the pre-Max days—before he ruined your life and I got married. We were wild and free. God, those were good times—the way our clothes reeked of smoke and spilt gin—the way we'd go to work hung over—the way we collected phone numbers on cocktail napkins of men we'd never call.
NICKY	I'm ready.

Nicky pulls her cell phone out of her purse and dials.

NICKY	I am really ready, Jessica.
JESSICA	Finally!
NICKY	I'm gonna go for it.
JESSICA	I am so happy to hear that, Nick! Who are you calling?
NICKY	(*Into the phone*) Max?
JESSICA	Who?
NICKY	(*On the phone*) Is this Max?

Beat.

Who?

    Beat.

I'm sorry. I think I have the wrong number. Sorry.

    Nicky hangs up the phone. A couple beats.

JESSICA	A relapse after nine months isn't really understandable but I'll pretend it didn't happen.
NICKY	(*Calmly*) I have been very good.
JESSICA	You have.
NICKY	I have not stalked, harassed or threatened. Have I?
JESSICA	Not once.
NICKY	I have successfully, and with great grace, I think, internalized the horror that I have been through.
JESSICA	The horror?
NICKY	I have smothered the urge to slash tires, to spy, to call and hang up, call and hang up—just to hear his voice— no, I have not done any of this. Not once. (*Embarrassed*) Why didn't you stop me!
JESSICA	I didn't know who you were calling.
NICKY	Would you have tried to stop me?
JESSICA	From making an ass of yourself? No.
NICKY	It's his birthday.
JESSICA	Don't cry.
NICKY	(*She's not crying*) I'm not.
JESSICA	You looked like you were going to cry.
NICKY	I am not crying!
JESSICA	Please—
NICKY	I'm fine—

JESSICA	Promise—
NICKY	I'm not even thinking about him—
JESSICA	Swear to me—
NICKY	I'm not gonna cry—
JESSICA	Oh no—
NICKY	Stop it!

Now she is welling up.

JESSICA	You are—
NICKY	Well, you keep saying it—
JESSICA	Your mascara—
NICKY	It's waterproof!
JESSICA	For God's sake—
NICKY	I just wanted to say happy birthday.
JESSICA	So say it.
NICKY	Happy birthday.
JESSICA	Good.
NICKY	Last year for his birthday I bought him—

She can't remember.

I bought him something for his birthday. God, it was really expensive, whatever it was. It wasn't the golf clubs. That was the year before.

JESSICA	Come on. Let me see you.

Nicky stands and turns in a circle.

JESSICA	You're fine.

| NICKY | I don't think I dialed the right number. |
| JESSICA | My husband is waiting in the car, Nicky. |

Nicky grabs her purse. Lights begin to fade to black.

NICKY	My God—what was that number?
JESSICA	Who cares.
NICKY	How can you be with a person for five years and forget their phone number?

Sound of car horn outside.

| JESSICA | (*Calling off*) Shut the fuck up! (*Now sweetly*) Ready? |

Jessica exits. As Nicky follows—

| NICKY | 276-0244? No-- 267-4420? That's not it. |

Black out.

The stage is still black in the interim, while the voice returns—

| **VOICE** | **One year and six months after the break up.** |

Nicky enters her apartment. She is carrying a Monet print. Jessica comes in behind her. Jessica plops down on the couch and rubs her own sore feet.

| NICKY | God, I love this. I mean it really resonated as soon as I saw it. I'm putting it over my bed, what do you think? |
| JESSICA | That's nice. |

NICKY	That's nice? That's it?
JESSICA	I think it's wonderful.
NICKY	So do I.
JESSICA	I need something for my head.
NICKY	Look in my purse.
JESSICA	Where is it?
NICKY	Here.

She hands her the purse. Jessica starts rummaging through. Instead she finds a condom.

JESSICA	What's this?
NICKY	What?
JESSICA	This.
NICKY	That's a condom.
JESSICA	I know it's a condom.
NICKY	You asked.
JESSICA	I mean what are you doing with it—what is this—as in what is this doing in your purse?
NICKY	Well, it didn't get along with the other condoms so I adopted it.
JESSICA	Who is this for?
NICKY	It's for me.
JESSICA	And?
NICKY	Dan.
JESSICA	Dan? Dan as in—he's-my-good-friend-and-I-could-never-sleep-with-him. Dan, who you met in a bar?
NICKY	Yes, that Dan. And I wouldn't have been in that bar had you not dragged me there to see the lavender ladies.
JESSICA	Oh good, I knew I could take the credit.

NICKY	Don't get so excited. I still have trouble sleeping with a man I met in a bar. Even if we have been friends for months.
JESSICA	So what does this mean?
NICKY	It means I like him.
JESSICA	I knew this would happen.
NICKY	Eventually—it doesn't take a rocket scientist.
JESSICA	Not that—not that you would have sex with an actual human being again—of course that was bound to happen—but that it happened with him. I saw it coming. I didn't say anything because it's not my place to interfere. I mean, it is—but I didn't want to predict it or maybe you would've pulled back.
NICKY	Jess, you are not my karmic guidance counselor, as much as you'd like to be. Things just happen and sometimes you have nothing to do with it.
JESSICA	I don't think so.
NICKY	I think so.
JESSICA	But this Dan thing—this is a good thing?
NICKY	I think so. I think it is a good thing.
JESSICA	That makes me happy.
NICKY	Me, too. Finally.

Lights begin to fade to black.

JESSICA	So?
NICKY	It's fine.
JESSICA	Not that it's all that matters.
NICKY	No, it's a small part of it.
JESSICA	But—
NICKY	All the time.
JESSICA	*All* the time?
NICKY	A lot.

JESSICA   Could you?

NICKY   I don't know yet.

              Black out.

              Black stage. The voice again—

VOICE   **Three years after the estrangement of Nicky and
              Max.**

                     *Lights come up on Nicky's apartment. A man's blazer
                     is thrown over the couch. A man's shoes are also on the
                     floor near the couch.*

                     Nicky's cell phone rings.

                     *Nicky comes out from the bedroom. She is putting on
                     earrings. She is dressed to go out.*

NICKY   *(Calling to bedroom)* Our reservations are at seven, Dan.

                     She answers her phone.

              Hello.

                     Beat.

              Hello?

                     Beat.

              Hello? Is anyone there? Hello?!

She waits a couple beats.

Listen, you ass hole, call me one more time and I'm calling the police!

Beat.

What? Who is this?

Beat.

Oh my God. You're calling me? That's been you—all those hang ups? All that bizarre heavy breathing? Really?

Listening. Very calm.

I hear what you're saying and I'm hanging up now, Max.

Nicky hangs up. She is in shock. She looks to the bedroom and calls off—

These hang ups are getting old. I'm changing my phone number!

Sudden commotion outside her door. Jessica enters very cool and composed. Too much so. It's almost scary.

Jessica holds the gun she took from Nicky. In the other hand, she holds papers.

JESSICA (*In a sort of cool shock*) Good evening, Nicky.

NICKY	(*Immediately senses something*) What happened?
JESSICA	(*Throws down papers—but stays a little smug*) He wants a divorce.
NICKY	A what?
JESSICA	It was one of those women.
NICKY	Who?
JESSICA	With the lavender hair.
NICKY	My God—which one?
JESSICA	I don't know which one!
NICKY	But—
JESSICA	Yes, she's older than him.
NICKY	But—
JESSICA	That's right! She's an old, dried up rocker with wrinkly tattoos. She's (*gestures with quotes*) "interesting" and "self-aware."
NICKY	Give me the gun.
JESSICA	For two years, he's been seeing her. Where was I?
NICKY	Okay—give me the gun!
JESSICA	(*Thinking about it*) Actually I was over here a lot.
NICKY	God, Jess, give me the gun!
JESSICA	Oh, take it. I'm through with it.
NICKY	What does that mean?

Nicky takes the gun from Jessica.

JESSICA	I shot his Porsche. The pig.
NICKY	Oh God. Okay, and yes, he is a pig.
JESSICA	But I'll tell you something—
NICKY	What?
JESSICA	I'll tell you—
NICKY	Yeah?
JESSICA	Something.

NICKY	What? What is it!
JESSICA	(*Very calmly*) Had I not set you up with that guy—
NICKY	Which guy?
JESSICA	The blind date. The perfect blind date. I'm sure you recall it.
NICKY	What are you talking about?
JESSICA	He was perfect after all. And I, Nicky, am *not* too damaged for perfect.
NICKY	You're kidding.
JESSICA	I'm not. And I thank you. Had you not sent me for those sunglasses—
NICKY	That was almost three years ago!
JESSICA	Three wonderful years. Thank God.
NICKY	How could you not tell me?
JESSICA	How could I get a word in edgewise?
NICKY	I admit it was a hard time.
JESSICA	Yes, it was. Your hard time was hard on all of us. But it's come together according to some rather twisted and perverse divine plan. You get over Max and end up with your very good friend Dan. The sex isn't as hot but he treats you like a queen. I—on the other hand—have had great sex with an adoring man—not my husband—for two and a half years until recently out of guilt, and now I'm thinking insanity, I broke it off. Yes, by a sheer act of will, of inhuman resolve, of disgusting fortitude—only to find out my husband has been having an affair with a woman with purple hair.
	So, after riddling his Porsche with bullets, I came here to return your gun, your now empty gun. I never really believed in guns but this one came in handy. So having said all that—have a wonderful time tonight wherever you're going.

Jessica begins to exit with great dignity. She turns back to Nicky—

By the way, there is nothing quite so wonderful as sleeping diagonally in your own bed or as liberating as walking around the house in your underwear with no one staring at your cellulite or saying 'while you're down there can you get me some water.' Why didn't you tell me how perfectly fine it is to be alone?

NICKY   Because I knew that as soon as I got too content, another one would come along and suck me back in. Misery is the perfect repellent.

JESSICA   Very tricky! I like it. I like it!

Jessica exits laughing maniacally. Nicky still holds the gun.

Lights begin to fade to black. Nicky looks at the gun and her cell phone and smiles at how far she's come.

And final black out.

THE OTHER SIDE OF MEANING

THE OTHER SIDE OF MEANING

Kristen Lazarian

[JOE & EMILY]

> *JOE and EMILY are leaving a graduate night class on the Romantic Poets.*

> *They are both in their twenties. Joe is dressed in trendy jeans and a tee shirt. He has on glasses that almost make him look like an intellectual. Emily is also in jeans and wearing a black leather jacket. Her hair is pulled back off her face.*

> *Lights come up as Joe and Emily come out of class. Joe holds the door open for Emily.*

EMILY   Thank you.

JOE   So what do you think?

EMILY   About what?

JOE   Class.

EMILY   I enjoy Keats but I like Coleridge better. Blake's in a category all his own—although it sort of defeats the purpose to even try to categorize him. And Shelley. Well, we all know his wife was really the brilliant one. You?

JOE   I have to take this class.

EMILY   Oh. See ya later.

> *She begins to leave.*

JOE   Wanna get a beer?

EMILY   What?

JOE	I know it's last minute.
EMILY	Have we ever talked? It's odd that you would suddenly want to drink beer with me.
JOE	I've been meaning to talk to you for awhile now.
EMILY	That's interesting, Mike.
JOE	It's Joe.
EMILY	(*Embarrassed*) I'm sorry. Mike's the guy with the flat top who sits next to you.
JOE	I hate formal introductions.
EMILY	Me, too.
JOE	And anyway, I know your name.
EMILY	Emily.
JOE	I know.
EMILY	And you are Joe. Hi.
JOE	I'm trying to impress you.
EMILY	Excuse me?
JOE	I'm trying to—
EMILY	You mean embarrass me.
JOE	No. Not at all.
EMILY	Well, I've been meaning to apologize to you.
JOE	Already? I don't know if that's a good sign.
EMILY	For staring... in class... I didn't mean to stare at you.
JOE	You were staring? At me?
EMILY	I confessed, alright? Don't pretend you didn't see me.
JOE	Okay. I confess, too. I saw you. It made me uncomfortable but intrigued.
EMILY	That's not what I meant by—
JOE	Don't tell me it was spit dangling from my lower lip.
EMILY	That's disgusting. Look, I've gotta run.
JOE	Where? This isn't fair. You stare at me in class and now you refuse me an explanation.
EMILY	It's very hard to explain.

JOE	Wait a minute. You have a reason? You don't even know me and you have a reason for avoiding me?
EMILY	It's not what you think I mean. Really.
JOE	What then?
EMILY	You remind me of someone, okay? I've gotta go now.
JOE	I do?
EMILY	Someone I should forget. Someone I thought I had forgotten until I saw you.
JOE	I see.
EMILY	Don't take it personally.
JOE	How can I not take it personally? I was born me only to remind you of him. And here I thought we could be great friends.
EMILY	I'm sorry, Joe.
JOE	Tell me who.
EMILY	I told you who.
JOE	Someone you need to forget isn't good enough.
EMILY	You remind me of a very evil and wicked person.
JOE	Now that's romantic.
EMILY	A very cruel, vindictive and deceitful person.
JOE	We're getting somewhere.
EMILY	Whenever I think of this person I get a sharp pain in the back of my neck that runs all the way down my spine. And, therefore, every time—
JOE	You look at me, you get a sharp pain.
EMILY	You're catching on.
JOE	But you kept looking. You like pain.
EMILY	So I'm a little masochistic. It was nice to talk to you.
JOE	Wait—I didn't know it was possible to break someone's heart without ever speaking a word to that person.
EMILY	I never said my heart was broken.
JOE	I can see it.

EMILY	You can?
JOE	Sure. In your eyes. They're her eyes actually.
EMILY	Who's this?
JOE	Emily, if I look like someone you used to know and remind you of him... well... just think how I could totally alter the meaning of that past relationship. Just because of the way I look.
EMILY	No, you would strip all the meaning away because you would end up being yourself.
JOE	I'll try to be him then!
EMILY	Impossible... and ridiculous.
JOE	Do that again.
EMILY	What?
JOE	When you tilt your head back like that and smile.
EMILY	Sorry, I can't do that on cue.
JOE	It was exactly like her. First the eyes and then the expression.
EMILY	What are you talking about?
JOE	You should know. I was attracted to you for the same reason that you were lusting after me.
EMILY	Did I say lust? I thought I said disgust.
JOE	You're just like her.
EMILY	Nice try but totally unoriginal. Goodbye.
JOE	I think you can redeem her memory.
EMILY	That would be way too much to ask of anyone.
JOE	It would help me.
EMILY	I really remind you of someone you knew?
JOE	And loved.
EMILY	Loved?
JOE	It's more than the way you look, Em. You have her spirit... it's deep and unsettling. Must be the eyes.
EMILY	I'm beginning to get the feeling that you have a strange knack for turning things around.

JOE	I can also do inside out. If it means enough to me.
EMILY	You don't know me. I couldn't possibly mean something to you.
JOE	She did.
EMILY	I'm sorry.
JOE	There's something you can do.
EMILY	I can't redeem her memory, Joe.
JOE	You don't think so?
EMILY	Your expectations of me will be too high.
JOE	You only have to be yourself... which is *her*. I'm sure of it.
EMILY	You look like him, you talk like him, you laugh like him. And you're beginning to look at me—the way— please. I have to go.
JOE	I will be him. Only better. If you'll let me. Please let me.
EMILY	You're confusing me.
JOE	But it's so simple. I'll be him. You'll be her. We'll right all the past wrongs. We'll say the things we wish we'd said. We'll forgive each other. Our relationship will have another meaning.
EMILY	We'll give new life to an old context.
JOE	We'll give old life to a new context.
EMILY	Okay.
JOE	Okay?
EMILY	I'm all for undoing the past when the chance comes along.
JOE	You mean it?
EMILY	And even for living happily ever after.
JOE	I've always wanted to live happily ever after.
EMILY	If not happily ever before.
JOE	It really wasn't.
EMILY	Which is the scary thing.

JOE	It scares me more to let you go. Now can we get a beer?
EMILY	She liked beer?
JOE	I thought so.
EMILY	Because I prefer wine.
JOE	Cabernet.
EMILY	Chardonnay.
JOE	I like chardonnay. We'll go to the Grill—
EMILY	That's where we used to go. I have a bottle in the fridge.
JOE	That's even better.
EMILY	That's what I thought.

Beat.

JOE	I missed you.

Joe and Emily take hands and—
Black Out

BEACH BALLS

BEACH BALLS

Kristen Lazarian

[ZOE & MEL, MARTIN, MIKE, MICKEY, MORRIS, MATT, MARK]

> *ZOE sits on a beach chair, stage center. She is in beachwear—a bathing suit or a bikini top and shorts. She wears sunglasses and has a bag of tanning oil and other accessories next to her chair. She reads **Anna Karenina**.*
>
> *A volleyball bounces past her. She continues reading without paying much attention.*
>
> *MEL enters looking for the ball. He is in swimming trunks, barefoot.*

ZOE	Over there.
MEL	I know.
ZOE	Excuse me for helping.

> *Mel goes and gets the ball.*

Watch the sand, Bozo.

MEL	What'd you call me?
ZOE	Bozo. As in the clown.
MEL	I know who Bozo the Clown is.
ZOE	A blood relative?
MEL	I was adopted.

ZOE	(*Growing irritation*) You don't say.
MEL	I know who my birth mother is.
ZOE	I can't imagine who.
MEL	You've probably seen her.
ZOE	Probably not.
MEL	Heard of Madonna?
ZOE	Madonna's your mother?
MEL	Her name *is* Madonna, isn't it?
ZOE	Somehow I never took her name literally.
MEL	You're supposed to.
ZOE	Whatever. She's *your* mom.
MEL	I'm kidding. I don't even like Madonna.
ZOE	I love her. She's underrated, misunderstood and totally cool. If she's blasphemous it's against patriarchy, certainly not God. And pushing the bounds of sexual expression is only a necessary means of defiance against the ways in which the good old boy's club attempts to control *and* disempower women, reducing them to sexual objects—or as in your fantasy, the saintly mothers of more men.
MEL	Hey wait. Don't insult men. I'm a man.
ZOE	Okay.
MEL	You noticed? Then maybe—maybe we could have dinner sometime. Do you cook?
ZOE	I'd rather fuck myself then cook you dinner. But thanks.
MEL	Okay.

> Mel exits as another volleyball comes out from stage
> left and rolls past Zoe, who tries to read her book.

> MARTIN enters looking for the ball. Zoe doesn't
> look at him or the ball. She reads her book.

ZOE	(*Reading*) Over there.
MARTIN	Where?
ZOE	There.
MARTIN	Where?
ZOE	Oh sorry. That wasn't a volleyball. That was an albino midget doing somersaults.
MARTIN	Really?
ZOE	Fuck off.
MARTIN	Okay.

Martin grabs the volleyball and exits.

Zoe reads. She is content. Until another volleyball passes her chair. She watches it, irritated, and then goes back to her book.

MIKE enters looking for his ball.

ZOE	Didn't see it.
MIKE	What?
ZOE	Didn't see the ball go by.
MIKE	How could you? You're reading.
ZOE	I'm so glad you noticed.
MIKE	Don't mind me.

Mike goes for the ball and grabs it.

ZOE	I don't yet.
MIKE	What's the book?
ZOE	Just a little ditty about love, war, passion, rejection, and suicide.
MIKE	Yeah? Sounds good.

ZOE	I laughed. I cried.
MIKE	Contemplated the meaning of life?
ZOE	Not yet.
MIKE	I have.
ZOE	Have you?
MIKE	Yes, and it can be summed up in one phrase which I stole from Shakespeare and then distorted—
ZOE	You know Shakespeare?
MIKE	Vaguely.
ZOE	Good enough.
MIKE	This is the meaning of life. To fuck or not to fuck.
ZOE	That's not Shakespeare. That's Mamet.
MIKE	No. It's mine. Based loosely on Shakespeare.
ZOE	Sort of makes me see Hamlet in a whole new light.
MIKE	To fuck or not to fuck.
ZOE	Amazing. And so romantic. Why didn't I think of that?
MIKE	I don't fucking know.
ZOE	Well, fuck.
MIKE	Who's Mamet?
ZOE	Okay. Get the fuck out.
MIKE	What'd I say?
ZOE	Get the fuck out of here. Go on, you fuck head.
MIKE	I'm going. Geez. Is Mamet your boyfriend?
ZOE	Get the fuck away from me.
MIKE	Okay. Okay.

Mike exits and another volleyball comes rolling out.

*MICKEY enters. He stops by Zoe's chair but she
ignores him and continues reading.*

MICKEY   See the ball?

ZOE   No. I'm reading. I have better things to do than look after your balls.

MICKEY   You've never seen my balls.

ZOE   Nor do I have any desire to do so.

MICKEY   Oh. You're one of those.

ZOE   Depends which day of the week.

MICKEY   Oooh. You're one of those.

ZOE   Why settle for 48 percent of the population when you crave the whole loaf of bread?

MICKEY   Wow. Can I watch?

ZOE   As long as you're confessing, I will, too. I'm actually a man.

MICKEY   *(Believes her)* A what?

ZOE   You think these are breasts, but I'm just another run-of-the-mill testosterone deficient, progesterone proficient XXY. I'm more than a man. I'm your basic chromosomal nightmare.

MICKEY   Like a freak. A mutant?

ZOE   Yeah. Like those turtles, but without the impulse toward senseless violence.

MICKEY   Well. I still think you're hot, whatever you are.

ZOE   That's very open minded of you.

MICKEY   Chicks must dig you.

ZOE   Exactly. Tender yet dominating. Sensitive yet firm. Insecure but charming. The perfect package.

MICKEY   So you're not into guys?

ZOE   Forty-eight percent of the time—yes, I am.

MICKEY   'Cause I'd take you out.

ZOE   Oh really?

MICKEY	If you didn't tell anyone.
ZOE	About you?
MICKEY	Yeah.
ZOE	Go fuck yourself.
MICKEY	Okay.

Mickey exits despondently. Zoe goes back to her book. She tries to read when yet another volleyball comes rolling past her.

MORRIS enters looking for the ball.

Zoe points in the direction it went without looking up from her book.

MORRIS	Hey, thanks.
ZOE	No problem.
MORRIS	Reading?
ZOE	No. I just stare at the pages while I fantasize about sex in the bathroom on airplanes.
MORRIS	No!
ZOE	Yeah.
MORRIS	That's one of *my* fantasies.
ZOE	No!
MORRIS	Yeah!
ZOE	(*So sarcastic*) Whoa—too weird.
MORRIS	That's just—wow—
ZOE	Cosmic.
MORRIS	All this time I thought I was the only one.
ZOE	There's probably thousands of us fake readers.
MORRIS	We should start a group.
ZOE	Fake readers anonymous.

MORRIS	But why be anonymous. We should be proud.
ZOE	I'm proud that I've been on page 52 of *Anna Karenina* for the last—

Checks her watch.

Three years now.

MORRIS	No way. Three years?
ZOE	Three years. Ten minutes. What's the difference? It's so easy to lose track of time when you're caught in the grip of ecstasy.
MORRIS	I've been there. I've been gripped.
ZOE	I can tell.
MORRIS	It's the Sunday paper. Does it every week. I'm totally gripped.
ZOE	I've never tried the Sunday paper.
MORRIS	This morning I was reading the sports section— next thing I know I'm in France, post-revolution, Marie Antoinette was going to the guillotine. She says to her loyal subjects, 'Let them eat cake.' And then she says to me— 'I'm not hungry for cake. I'm hungry for you.' So we go at it and I send her to her death satisfied *and* completely over Napoleon.
ZOE	Wow. The Sunday paper did *that*?
MORRIS	Last week—Cleopatra.
ZOE	Well, *everyone's* been with her.
MORRIS	But it was different with me.
ZOE	Funny how men think that.

He leans over, trying to read her book.

I'm getting turned on.

ZOE	Back off.
MORRIS	It's much better than the reality of sex.
ZOE	My reality is that you're bugging the fuck out of me.

She flips him off.

Grip this.

MORRIS	(*Wounded*) Oh. Okay.

Morris exits.

Zoe is at her wits end. She opens the book again but can hardly focus when one, two, three volleyballs roll by her.

MATT enters and looks around.

MATT	Have you seen my balls?
ZOE	No, but I've seen everyone else's. Do they look the same?
MATT	Large and round. Soft to the touch but firm and hard when tossed.
ZOE	Oh. Those balls. Over there.
MATT	Thanks.
ZOE	All of those yours?

Matt is retrieving his balls.

MATT	Yes, they are.

ZOE	I don't know what kind of a game you're playing but—
MATT	I play with myself. I'm a juggler.
ZOE	You juggle volleyballs?
MATT	Volleyballs. Tangerines. Steak knives.
ZOE	You must be very talented.
MATT	So, I've been told.
ZOE	Finely tuned.
MATT	Whatever it takes.
ZOE	To handle all those balls. And with bare feet.
MATT	It's good for grounding me.
ZOE	Which is good for juggling?
MATT	What's good for the juggler is good for the jester.
ZOE	(*Straight*) You made that up. Get out.
MATT	No, it's a well-known Celtic cliché. The Celts get very little credit for their clichés.
ZOE	I thought it was what's good for the goose is good for the gander.
MATT	That's the corrupted Franco text propagated by some chick with a fetish for birds.
ZOE	Yeah, probably the same *chick* who started that profound saying—fuck a duck.
MATT	I've juggled ducks.
ZOE	I'm sure.
MATT	I had feathers up my orifices for weeks.
ZOE	How would you like to have one of those balls up your orifices?
MATT	Your hostility is offensive and unbecoming.
ZOE	(*Smiles*) Thank you.

A volleyball comes flying out from offstage, hitting Zoe. Then another aimed at her, then another.

ZOE	(*Yelling off*) KNOCK IT OFF! Ouch!

> *Zoe starts throwing the balls back offstage. Matt tries to escape, dodging the balls. She throws one at him.*

MATT	Ahh. Watch it.
ZOE	(*Yelling offstage*) I have had one of the worst weeks of my entire life and all I wanted was to sit here in peace and read *Anna Karenina* so I could vicariously experience someone else's suicide—so I suggest you all fuck off and take your balls with you!
MATT	PMS?
ZOE	*That* is just the clinical term for honesty!
MATT	No.
ZOE	Goodbye. So long. Fuck off.
MATT	Okay—fine.

> *Matt exits.*

> *Zoe tries to calm down. She sits. She picks up her book. She reads.*

> *MARK enters carrying a ball. Zoe doesn't look up. She only grits her teeth.*

ZOE	I have no idea where it went!
MARK	I have it.
ZOE	Then hang on to it. I'm getting lethally irritated.
MARK	You don't want it back?
ZOE	That's not mine.
MARK	I saw you throw it—I thought—

Mel, Martin, Mike, Mickey, Morris, and Matt stand together—

MORRIS	That's my ball.
MARTIN	Is not.
MIKE	It's mine.
MEL	Yeah, right. Give it—
MORRIS	Right here—
MATT	Hey, wait. It's mine.
MICKEY	They're not all yours.
ZOE	(*To Mark*) Just toss it to the penis gallery.

Mark tosses the ball past them, offstage. They all scramble for it.

MARK	Good book?
ZOE	Are you serious?
MARK	Yeah. Are you?
ZOE	It's *Anna Karenina*.
MARK	Heavy.
ZOE	Very.
MARK	Tolstoy.
ZOE	(*Interested*) Very.
MARK	It's been awhile.
ZOE	You know it?
MARK	Of course, I know it. I used to have a deeper appreciation for Tolstoy. Until I found out he renounced his own wife.
ZOE	(*Mesmerized*) No kidding.
MARK	I have a graduate degree in Comparative Lit with an emphasis in early 20th Century Russian lyrical poetry. I did my thesis on Boris Pasternak but I

read my fair share of Tolstoy and Dostoevsky,
and some Chekhov—just for laughs.

> *Beat. Zoe stares at Mark dazed and in awe. True love.*

ZOE   Would you like to fuck?

> *Mark smiles at her warmly and with this we—*

Black Out

About the Playwright

Kristen Lazarian is an award-winning playwright who has had her full-length and short plays produced, work-shopped and stage-read at many venues in L.A. including the Geffen Playhouse, Theatre 40, East-West Players, Theatre Geo, the Road Theatre, Pacific Resident Theatre, 68 Cent Crew, and the Blank Theatre. Her plays have also been staged across the United States, including New York City. She has had productions internationally in Holland, England, Australia, and Canada. Her plays include *Push, Love Like Blue, Flesh & Tenderness, Inviting Karma, Sophisticated Barflies & Other Short Plays*, among others.

In addition to writing plays, Kristen is a screenwriter. She penned *The Shift*, based on the spiritual teachings of self-improvement pioneer Wayne Dyer. She is a writer and script consultant for the series *Tales of Everyday Magic* and has other works in development.

Kristen is a member of the Dramatist Guild and the Alliance of Los Angeles Playwrights. She lives in Los Angeles with her husband and their three sons.

Also by Kristen Lazarian

full length plays:

Love Like Blue

Push

Flesh & Tenderness

Inviting Karma

Good Grace

Between You & Me

other short plays:

Intimate Distances

Angel in the Attic

In the Church of the Pen

Spring Forgets

Imaginings

Bad News

My Name is Bridget

Harry & the Witch

Slow Burn